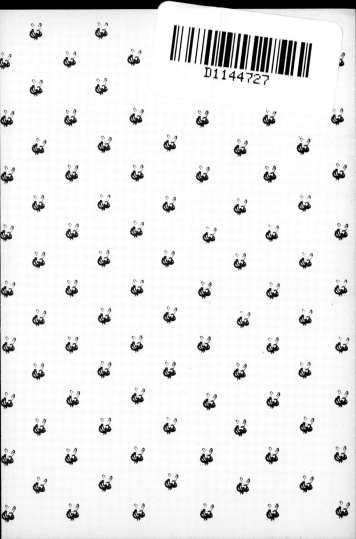

TIGGER
COMES TO THE
FOREST

TIGGER
COMES TO THE
FOREST

A.A. MILNE

illustrated by

ERNEST H. SHEPARD

TED SMART

TIGGER
COMES TO THE
FOREST

Winnie-the-Pooh woke up suddenly in the middle of the night and listened. Then he got out of bed, and lit his candle, and stumped across the room to see if anybody was trying to get into his honey-cupboard, and they weren't, so he stumped back again, blew out his candle, and got into bed. Then he heard the noise again.

'Is that you, Piglet?' he said.

But it wasn't.

'Come in, Christopher Robin,' he said.

But Christopher Robin didn't.

'Tell me about it to-morrow, Eeyore,' said Pooh sleepily.

But the noise went on.

'*Worraworraworraworraworra*,' said Whatever-it-was, and Pooh found that he wasn't asleep after all.

'What can it be?' he thought. 'There are lots of noises in the Forest, but this is a different one. It isn't a growl, and it isn't a purr, and it isn't a bark, and it isn't the noise-you-make-before-beginning-a-piece-of-poetry, but it's a noise of some kind, made by a strange animal! And he's making it outside my door. So I shall get up and ask him not to do it.'

He got out of bed and opened his front door.

'Hallo!' said Pooh, in case there was anything outside.

'Hallo!' said Whatever-it-was.

'Oh!' said Pooh. 'Hallo!'

'Hallo!'

'Oh, *there* you are!' said Pooh. 'Hallo!'

'Hallo!' said the Strange Animal, wondering how long this was going on.

Pooh was just going to say 'Hallo!' for the fourth time when he thought that he

wouldn't, so he said, 'Who is it?' instead.

'Me,' said a voice.

'Oh!' said Pooh. 'Well, come here.'

So Whatever-it-was came here, and in the light of the candle he and Pooh looked at each other.

'I'm Pooh,' said Pooh.

'I'm Tigger,' said Tigger.

'Oh!' said Pooh, for he had never seen an animal like this before. 'Does Christopher Robin know about you?'

'Of course he does,' said Tigger.

'Well,' said Pooh, 'it's the middle of the night, which is a good time for going to sleep. And to-morrow morning we'll have some honey for breakfast. Do Tiggers like honey?'

'They like everything,' said Tigger cheerfully.

'Then if they like going to sleep on the floor, I'll go back to bed,' said Pooh, 'and we'll do things in the morning. Good Night.'

And he got back into bed and went
fast asleep.

When he awoke in the morning, the first
thing he saw was Tigger, sitting in front
of the glass and looking at himself.

'Hallo!' said Pooh.

'Hallo!' said Tigger. 'I've found

somebody just like me. I thought I was the only one of them.'

Pooh got out of bed, and began to explain what a looking-glass was, but just as he was getting to the interesting part, Tigger said:

'Excuse me a moment, but there's something climbing up your table,' and with one loud *Worraworraworraworraworra* he jumped at the end of the tablecloth, pulled it to the ground, wrapped himself up in it three times, rolled to the other end of the room, and, after a terrible struggle, got his head into the daylight again, and said cheerfully: 'Have I won?'

'That's my tablecloth,' said Pooh, as he began to unwind Tigger.

'I wondered what it was,' said Tigger.

'It goes on the table and you put things on it.'

'Then why did it try to bite me when I wasn't looking?'

'I don't *think* it did,' said Pooh.

'It tried,' said Tigger, 'but I was too quick for it.'

Pooh put the cloth back on the table, and he put a large honey-pot on the cloth, and they sat down to breakfast. And as soon as they sat down, Tigger took a large mouthful

of honey . . . and he looked up at the ceiling with his head on one side, and made exploring

noises with his tongue, and considering
noises, and what-have-we-got-*here* noises . . .
and then he said in a very decided voice:

'Tiggers don't like honey.'

'Oh!' said Pooh, and tried to make it sound
Sad and Regretful. 'I thought they liked
everything.'

'Everything except honey,' said Tigger.

Pooh felt rather pleased about this, and
said that, as soon as he had finished his
own breakfast, he would take Tigger round to
Piglet's house, and Tigger could try some of
Piglet's haycorns.

'Thank you, Pooh,' said Tigger, 'because
haycorns is really what Tiggers like best.'

So after breakfast they went round to
see Piglet, and Pooh explained as they went
that Piglet was a Very Small Animal who
didn't like bouncing, and asked Tigger not to
be too Bouncy just at first. And Tigger,
who had been hiding behind trees and jumping
out on Pooh's shadow when it wasn't looking,

said that Tiggers were only bouncy before
breakfast, and that as soon as they had had
a few haycorns they became Quiet and Refined.
So by-and-by they knocked at the door of
Piglet's house.

'Hallo, Pooh,' said Piglet.

'Hallo, Piglet. This is Tigger.'

'Oh, is it?' said Piglet, and he edged
round to the other side of the table. 'I
thought Tiggers were smaller than that.'

'Not the big ones,' said Tigger.

'They like haycorns,' said Pooh, 'so that's what we've come for, because poor Tigger hasn't had any breakfast yet.'

Piglet pushed the bowl of haycorns towards Tigger, and said, 'Help yourself,' and then he got close up to Pooh and felt

much braver, and said, 'So you're Tigger? Well, well!' in a careless sort of voice. But Tigger said nothing because his mouth was full of haycorns. . . .

After a long munching noise he said:

'Ee-ers o i a-ors.'

And when Pooh and Piglet said, 'What?' he said, 'Skoos ee,' and went outside for a moment.

When he came back he said firmly:

'Tiggers don't like haycorns.'

'But you said they liked everything except honey,' said Pooh.

'Everything except honey *and* haycorns,' explained Tigger.

When he heard this, Pooh said, 'Oh, I see!' and Piglet, who was rather glad that Tiggers didn't like haycorns, said, 'What about thistles?'

'Thistles,' said Tigger, 'is what Tiggers like best.'

'Then let's go along and see Eeyore,' said Piglet.

So the three of them went; and after they had walked and walked and walked, they came to the part of the Forest where Eeyore was.

'Hallo, Eeyore!' said Pooh. 'This is Tigger.'

'What is?' said Eeyore.

'This,' explained Pooh and Piglet together, and Tigger smiled his happiest smile and said nothing.

Eeyore walked all round Tigger one way, and then turned and walked all round him the other way.

'What did you say it was?' he asked.

'Tigger.'

'Ah!' said Eeyore.

'He's just come,' explained Piglet.

'Ah!' said Eeyore again.

He thought for a long time and then said:

'When is he going?'

Pooh explained to Eeyore that Tigger was a great friend of Christopher Robin's, who had come to stay in the Forest, and Piglet explained to Tigger that he mustn't mind what Eeyore said because he was *always* gloomy; and Eeyore explained to Piglet that,

on the contrary, he was feeling particularly cheerful this morning; and Tigger explained to anybody who was listening that he hadn't had any breakfast yet.

'I knew there was something,' said Pooh. 'Tiggers always eat thistles, so that was why we came to see you, Eeyore.'

'Don't mention it, Pooh.'

'Oh, Eeyore, I didn't mean that I didn't *want* to see you—'

'Quite – quite. But your new stripy friend – naturally, he wants his breakfast. What did you say his name was?'

'Tigger.'

'Then come this way, Tigger.'

Eeyore led the way to the most thistly-looking patch of thistles that ever was, and waved a hoof at it.

'A little patch I was keeping for my birthday,' he said; 'but, after all, what *are* birthdays? Here to-day and gone to-morrow. Help yourself, Tigger.'

Tigger thanked him and looked a little anxiously at Pooh.

'Are these really thistles?' he whispered.

'Yes,' said Pooh.

'What Tiggers like best?'

'That's right,' said Pooh.

'I see,' said Tigger.

So he took a large mouthful, and he gave a large crunch.

'*Ow!*' said Tigger.

He sat down and put his paw in his mouth.

'What's the matter?' asked Pooh.

'*Hot!*' mumbled Tigger.

'Your friend,' said Eeyore, 'appears to have bitten on a bee.'

Pooh's friend stopped shaking his head to get the prickles out, and explained that Tiggers didn't like thistles.

'Then why bend a perfectly good one?' asked Eeyore.

'But you said,' began Pooh, '—you *said* that Tiggers liked everything except honey and haycorns.'

'*And* thistles,' said Tigger, who was now running round in circles with his tongue hanging out.

Pooh looked at him sadly.

'What are we going to do?' he asked Piglet.

Piglet knew the answer to that, and he said at once that they must go and see Christopher Robin.

'You'll find him with Kanga,' said Eeyore.

He came close to Pooh, and said in
a loud whisper:

'*Could* you ask your friend to do his
exercises somewhere else? I shall be
having lunch directly, and don't want it
bounced on just before I begin. A trifling
matter, and fussy of me, but we all have our
little ways.'

Pooh nodded solemnly and called to Tigger.

'Come along and we'll go and see Kanga.
She's sure to have lots of breakfast for you.'

Tigger finished his last circle and came
up to Pooh and Piglet.

'Hot!' he explained with a large and friendly smile. 'Come on!' and he rushed off.

Pooh and Piglet walked slowly after him. And as they walked Piglet said nothing, because he couldn't think of anything, and Pooh said nothing, because he was thinking of a poem. And when he had thought of it he began:

What shall we do about poor little Tigger?
If he never eats nothing he'll never get bigger.
He doesn't like honey and haycorns and thistles
Because of the taste and because of the bristles.
And all the good things which an animal likes
Have the wrong sort of swallow or too many
      spikes.

'He's quite big enough anyhow,' said Piglet.

'He isn't *really* very big.'

'Well, he *seems* so.'

Pooh was thoughtful when he heard this, and then he murmured to himself:

> But whatever his weight in pounds,
>   shillings, and ounces,
> He always seems bigger because
>   of his bounces.

'And that's the whole poem,' he said. 'Do you like it, Piglet?'

'All except the shillings,' said Piglet. 'I don't think they ought to be there.'

'They wanted to come in after the pounds,' explained Pooh, 'so I let them. It is the best way to write poetry, letting things come.'

'Oh, I didn't know,' said Piglet.

Tigger had been bouncing in front of them all this time, turning round every now and then to ask, 'Is this the way?' – and now at last they came in sight of Kanga's house, and there was Christopher Robin. Tigger rushed up to him.

'Oh, there you are, Tigger!' said Christopher Robin. 'I knew you'd be somewhere.'

'I've been finding things in the Forest,' said Tigger importantly. 'I've found a pooh and a piglet and an eeyore, but I can't find any breakfast.'

Pooh and Piglet came up and hugged Christopher Robin, and explained what had been happening.

'Don't *you* know what Tiggers like?' asked Pooh.

'I expect if I thought very hard I should,'

said Christopher Robin, 'but I *thought* Tigger knew.'

'I do,' said Tigger. 'Everything there is in the world except honey and haycorns and – what were those hot things called?'

'Thistles.'

'Yes, and those.'

'Oh, well then, Kanga can give you some breakfast.'

So they went into Kanga's house, and when Roo had said 'Hallo, Pooh' and 'Hallo, Piglet' once, and 'Hallo, Tigger' twice, because he had never said it before and it sounded funny, they told Kanga what they wanted, and Kanga said very kindly, 'Well, look in my cupboard, Tigger dear, and see what you'd like.' Because she knew at once that, however big Tigger seemed to be, he wanted as much kindness as Roo.

'Shall I look, too?' said Pooh, who was

beginning to feel a little eleven o'clockish. And he found a small tin of condensed milk, and something seemed to tell him

that Tiggers didn't like this, so he took it into a corner by itself, and went with it to see that nobody interrupted it.

But the more Tigger put his nose into this and his paw into that, the more things

he found which Tiggers didn't like. And when
he had found everything in the cupboard,
and couldn't eat any of it, he said to
Kanga, 'What happens now?'

But Kanga and Christopher Robin and
Piglet were all standing round Roo, watching
him have his Extract of Malt. And Roo
was saying, 'Must I?' and Kanga was saying,
'Now, Roo dear, you remember what you
promised.'

'What is it?' whispered Tigger to
Piglet.

'His Strengthening Medicine,' said Piglet.
'He hates it.'

So Tigger came closer, and he leant over
the back of Roo's chair, and suddenly he
put out his tongue, and took one large
golollop, and, with a sudden jump of surprise,

Kanga said, 'Oh!' and then clutched at the
spoon again, just as it was disappearing, and
pulled it safely back out of Tigger's mouth.
But the Extract of Malt had gone.

'Tigger *dear*!' said Kanga.

'He's taken my medicine, he's taken my
medicine, he's taken my medicine!' said Roo
happily, thinking it was a tremendous joke.

Then Tigger looked up at the ceiling, and
closed his eyes, and his tongue went round

and round his chops, in case he had left any outside, and a peaceful smile came over his face as he said, 'So *that's* what Tiggers like!'

Which explains why he always lived at Kanga's house afterwards, and had Extract of Malt for breakfast, dinner, and tea. And sometimes, when Kanga thought he wanted strengthening, he had a spoonful or two of Roo's breakfast after meals as medicine.

'But *I* think,' said Piglet to Pooh, 'that he's been strengthened quite enough.'

Tigger Comes to the Forest
is taken from *The House at Pooh Corner*
originally published in Great Britain 11th October 1928
by Methuen & Co. Ltd.
Text by A.A.Milne and line drawings by Ernest H.Shepard
copyright under the Berne Convention

First published 1991 by Methuen Children's Books
an imprint of Egmont Children's Books Limited
239 Kensington High Street, London W8 6SA

This edition first produced in 1998 for The Book People
Hall Wood Avenue, Haydock, St Helens WA11 9UL

ISBN 1 85613 464 4

3 5 7 9 10 8 6 4

Printed in Hong Kong